KDP BOOKS

Sacred Hearts

Sacred Hearts is the third novel written by Imogen R
Clarice (2018) and *Violet Minded* (2019). Alongside her literary work, Imogen has written and directed several short films, including *Mia's World* (2022) and *Othering* (2020). She holds an MA in Script Writing from Goldsmiths, University of London and is currently studying for an MSc in Psychotherapy at the Metanoia Institute in London. In addition to its publication as a novella, *Sacred Hearts* has also been adapted as a feature film script, and has been made into a short film, *Three of Swords* (2024).

KDP BOOKS

First published worldwide in 2024 by KDP Books in partnership with Amazon.

www.kdp.com

Copyright © 2024 Imogen Radwan

All rights reserved

IBSN: 9798334986985

Imogen Radwan

SACRED HEARTS

KDP Books

foreword

capital letters: a parable

after six years of ambivalence towards capital letters, i finally turned off auto-caps on my phone and the decision has been eating me alive. now i look like someone who has gone the extra mile to appear nonchalant (and i have), but the worst thing is that if i go back and change it that's gonna require even more effort, so i guess now we're just stuck with it and anyone reading this is lucky that i wrote sacred hearts before making such a life-altering decision.

Foreword 2.0

August 2024

After six years of writing this book, it wasn't until the day of publication — as I sat down to proofread the foreword I'd read a hundred times over — that I found myself recoiling at the words before me. *I can't publish this*, I thought, *this isn't even how I feel anymore*. Ironically, that exact thought was the original message of the foreword regarding *Sacred Hearts* itself. It was like opening a Russian doll, where each figure inside tells you the one before got it wrong, only to reveal another doll inside that correcting the last.

    For six years, *Sacred Hearts* has weighed on me in this way. As I've grown older, I've become more distant from Marie — who is really someone I used to be. I simply didn't think that a novel started then could not be completed now, because the author has fundamentally changed. And yet, for all my distance from it, I can't bear the idea of not publishing this work. There's still a part of me, and some delusional, limerent undercurrent running through this prose, that knows it's a story worth telling; and it's a story that won't rest until it is told.

I have been sitting on *Sacred Hearts* since 2018. In that time, a series of short films, creative projects, day jobs, relationships, moves, pandemics, wars and genocides have all contributed to a growing sense that the narrative itself has evolved. I suppose there's a part of me that believes that in the 2020s, the only way to create is experimentally, tenuously, with the knowledge that our work is as precarious as the world from which it was borne. When the future is so uncertain, perhaps writing requires a fluidity, an ambiguity that can exist amid the vagaries of our time. And with any luck, perhaps our art will survive.

I started this year spending a lot of time alone, having moved back to London after a not-so-great year in Brighton. When I first returned, I was commuting ninety minutes from one side of the city to the other, which was intensely isolating. On my way up, I would practice mindfulness, acquainting myself with the route from south to north // two worlds separated and united by a formidable river. On the way back down, late night country ballads soothed against the low howl of trains roaring through the night, wires cutting across the sky smudged with cloud, illuminated by polluted moonlight. At midnight, on my walk home from the station, I would listen to Tibetan bowls, sonorous beneath the heavy moon which hung over a house opposite the park; the house felt unreal, like a cardboard cut-out, a shadow-house. That's how a lot of life felt to me at the time — as if a veneer had been stripped back, and I was being shown something beneath the layers of reality. The world of images and symbols no longer made any sense to me.

but then the summer came and changed all of that. i was overcome with extraversion. i wanted to be outside, and busy. i made friends again, and *brat* came out and i downloaded hinge and thought about moving back east and then i turned off auto-caps and before i knew it i was at a rave and waking up at 3pm before going to hampstead heath to make out with a guy who insisted on being friends as if he knew what that meant, so i bought a solo ticket to see mitski in victoria park singing about how lonely she was and realised that perhaps i had not changed at all in the past six years.

You see, in the original foreword I'd written that *Sacred Hearts* exists in an earlier evolutionary phase that I no longer felt equipped to inhabit — but I don't know if that's totally true. One thing I've learnt about being human is that our lives are often spent shifting between two opposing poles of the self, in an endless pursuit of equilibrium. That said, *Sacred Hearts* is still a story which belongs decisively to my own past. It's one I'd like to free myself of, and all of the suffering that it holds — even if it's not technically 'perfect' or as good as some of my more recent writing.

In spite of this, it might also be the best thing I have ever written, because in all truth — it is probably the most universal. And while I do hold some ambivalence towards this work, and many other things, I have decided to share it in its current form. As we all change, so too does the art, adjusting to our ever-shifting perspective.

How is it over there?
How lonely is it?
Is it still glowing red at sunset?
Are the birds still singing on
The way to the forest?

Lee Chang-dong, 'Agnes' Song' (2010)

Part I

I

I was thinking about how life is a series of concentric circles, starting with the universe and ending with the self. People always say that the world doesn't revolve around you, but it does — it does every time and without fail. It was silent in the apartment, pitch black and very cold. Anna was in her room, probably sleeping, and I most likely would have been asleep too had I not been thinking so much.

I wanted to find a way to be happy on my own, without needing to rely on anyone else for that happiness. For a long time I thought it would be impossible to do that; you see, other people were my reason for living. How lonely and dull a world it would be if you were the only person in it! I suppose that's why for me it followed naturally that I couldn't be happy by myself. It was true that I liked to do things alone; I walked alone, read alone, watched films alone, ate and slept alone; in short, I enjoyed my own company. But it was never long before I would begin to feel the pangs of loneliness creeping up again. And although I had known the pleasures of sex, these people always had somewhere else to be in the end. I soon learnt that regardless of your own feelings, people will come and go as they please; it is just what they do, and at the end of the day you are by yourself, once again at the centre of the concentric circles that comprise the universe.

It is hard, when you really think about it, to accept that you might spend the majority of your life in isolation; you might end up living alone, working by yourself, or stuck with people who don't understand you. If only there were a way, I thought, of being one's own soulmate; if only you understood yourself better than you did, and knew exactly what to do or say to make yourself feel better. You could not find such a person in someone else, I knew that much. People are too caught up in their own problems to know how to treat another in the way they need to be treated. You have to spend a lot of time with someone to learn how to do that — and even then, you can get it wrong sometimes.

As I turned over in bed, I found myself smiling uncontrollably. With the duvet over my head, I continued to smile as I found myself being kissed on the lips by the person lying beside me. His lips were gentle yet powerful; it was a kiss of ecstasy, of desire fulfilled, and at that precise moment I knew I had fallen in love.

'Marie,' he said, 'what were you thinking about?'

'Oh, this and that,' I replied. 'It's Sunday tomorrow. Maybe we can go to the park?'

'Yes,' he said, 'that would be nice.' He kissed me again before I turned over and tried to sleep, this time without thinking too much.

His name is Valentine, 'Val' for short, and we had fallen for each other very quickly; in spite of all the thoughts running through my head that night, I loved him without reserve, as a man loves his religion, with absolute faith and certainty. I sunk back into his arms, blissful, like I had somehow defied the fact of our separateness.

The next morning I was sat up in bed with Val beside me. It was ten o'clock and I could hear Anna walking around on the landing, the old floorboards groaning beneath her slow steps towards the bathroom; the door closed; I heard the hum and sprinkling of the shower.

Would you like some coffee? I heard myself say, pulling my hair into a bun. I could feel his eyes resting upon my back as I put on my robe, making a show of slipping my arms gracefully through the satin sleeves, pulling the garment over my body and tying it at the waist in a bow. It is vanity, yes, but I am from Paris, a city of mirrors, where before you see us we have already seen ourselves reflected ten times.

Perhaps it is misleading to say I am from Paris. I was born here to a French mother and an English father. They had crossed paths one day outside the Sacré-Coeur. She was eighteen and a student at the time, but she had recently started acting in films after catching the attention of a particular director of the New Wave. My father was twenty-five and a linguistics student in London, but had saved up enough to spend the summer travelling Europe. As many young men before him had been, he was captivated by the sight of my mother — an exceptionally beautiful woman with large blue eyes that drank up the skies, and skin that had never seen a blemish in its life. As my father recounted it, he was seized by a sudden desire to speak to her, and struck up a conversation about the book she was reading (it was Françoise Sagan's *Bonjour Tristesse* — which had actually been given to her by another man, who had written her an endearing inscription on the first page, before dumping her two weeks later). The way he recalled this episode always made it sound like something out of a fairytale; that the attraction was instant and inexplicable, that it must have been love at first sight. I was more than happy to believe it. It was a match made only in Paris, and soon enough my father got it into his head that in order for things to work out, he would have to leave England for good. Nine years later I was born at the Robert-Debré hospital in the 19th arrondissement, and lived the first year of my life in France.

When I was one year old my mother committed suicide. I have imagined and replayed the scene repeatedly in my mind, trying to die vicariously through her; to imagine what the weather had been like, and if the sun had been behind her. I wondered whether she had been listening to music or silence, or perhaps the gentle lull of birdsong; what had clothes she worn on the day she decided to depart? What were her final thoughts? I wondered what words she had graced the world with as she looked one last time at the colossal, unwavering sky, and if she felt fear, sadness, an immense freedom, or simply the absence of any feeling. She had left no note, no clues as to why she had committed this ultimate act of negation. I knew she had suffered from depression after I was born, but that was all the information I had. I was too young to remember the months leading up to her death, and have been left only with fragments of a life lived primarily on the screen; a life so remote from whoever my mother was when the cameras were not rolling. I have so little to tell me why she did what she did.

Of course, Paris immediately became tainted for my father. The city was abruptly plunged into darkness, pushing us back across the channel and to a tiny village in Oxfordshire, severing all ties from the past. I spent the rest of my childhood in England, never quite feeling at home, for reasons I couldn't understand at the time. We were not rich, and in all my years growing up I couldn't name a single job that my father held down for more than a couple of months. He considered himself different from most people, and struggled to find employment that he deemed meaningful enough to pursue. He would take on sporadic work as a supply teacher, and enjoyed education because he said it gave him hope every time a student asked him why they had to learn something. He often said that *why* is the only question worth asking.

Many times in my childhood I found myself returning to the question of why. Every time something didn't turn out in the way I had hoped — when I was disliked among my peers, for example — all I could do was ask why. The children at the village school never quite allowed me to fit in, but the reason was never clear. I knew their parents must have told them about my mother. I wouldn't be surprised if her death had been presented as a sudden existential whim, as if she had just woken up one day and decided to do it. Or perhaps that's exactly how it happened — the outcome is the same either way.

On the other hand, my father's strangeness, his separateness from the other parents, made me an object of ridicule at school. He had a habit of taking me to graveyards when I was younger, bringing a portable voice recorder with him which he believed could pick up frequencies from beyond. These frequencies were called electronic voice phenomena, or EVPs.

Marie, he would say, his forefinger hovering over his lips, signalling for me to be quiet. And I would fall silent as he pressed 'record' and spoke softly, unnaturally, into the microphone, as if he himself were a ghost. I was terrified — not of the supernatural, but of him; because I knew even at the age of four or five that he had been irrevocably changed by my mother's passing.

When I was five, he took me to the graveyard where my mother is buried. I remember it like a dream; trees rustling in sunlight and breeze, the soft edges of memory and unreality, weathered tombstones dotted about the grass. We were standing in front of her grave. *In loving memory of Julie Lovell. 1968-1997.* My father did his usual ritual of bringing his forefinger to his lips and signalling silence, before pressing 'record' and waiting.

Hello, Julie, he said, his voice distant and detached. *If you can hear us Julie...say "hello."* I feel a shudder in my spinal cord — a delayed response perhaps. Perhaps for the dead, there is no concept of time, and a *hello* spoken years ago may be the same as a *hello* remembered now.

Upon my father's words, I looked up from her grave. I observed my surroundings; the tall cedar trees, the old stone church in the distance, the long, unkempt grass.

Hello, Julie, he repeated.

In the threshold of the church, I could just make out a tall figure standing in the shade. I wondered if he had been there the whole time.

How are you today, Julie? I'm here with Marie today. Say hello, Marie.

The figure — a man, surely — didn't appear to be moving.

Marie, my father said, snapping his fingers in front of me.

Hello, I said; but the words felt disembodied and mechanical, as if my voice were coming

from outside myself. I turned back to him. I wanted to tell him that I was scared, but he

simply held up his hand.

I know you're here with us, Julie. Please give us a sign, to let us know you're listening.

I looked back towards the church and the man was gone. I had frozen on the spot, but my father failed to notice. Instead, he continued to solicit the my mother to finish a sequence of alphabet letters for him: *A...B...C...D...* As if her being able to say the letter E would bridge the gulf between them.

From within the trees, a strange, indistinct breeze filled the space between the leaves, the grass and the sky.

A...B...C...D... my father's voice continued; but all I could think about was the man's sudden absence.

I decided to name this figure the Tall Man. It was a name which required no thought, no effort of the imagination to clearly identify his presence. In naming him, I could also stay vigilant in case he appeared again — whether in a sunlit churchyard or stood in the corner of my bedroom, like in those videos on the internet. For years to come I strongly feared that he might suddenly arise from the gloom and drag me to some dark, terrible place, and it wasn't long before he became a recurring figure in my dreams.

It is perhaps to be expected that my father's strange behaviour in graveyards hindered any chance I had of fitting in at school. I have a distinct memory of being surrounded by my peers, as Miss Holmes regarded me at the front of the class with the words 'Show and Tell' written on the board. In my outstretched palm I held my father's tape recorder, my classmates staring at it as if it were a loaded gun. I can still feel the discomfort now, and my desperate glances towards Miss Holmes for support, my feeble voice saying:

This weekend we went ghost-hunting in the graveyard. This is a tape recorder, which my dad

uses to pick up EVPs.

I quickly ran out of words. Someone whispered to somebody else. They laughed.

Well that's exciting, isn't it? Miss Holmes chimed in, betraying no sign of dismay whatsoever. *Did you have fun?*

I was too distracted by the whispering to answer. I heard another giggle. Miss Holmes shushed the class and told everybody that it is rude not to listen when someone is speaking. But I couldn't go on; I just stared at the floor, waiting for it to dissipate beneath me. Something hit the side of my face; I looked down and saw a crumpled ball of paper at my feet as a great torrent of laughter rippled from the back of the room to where I stood. One child was quick to make a mock ghost noise, like something from a pantomime. Soon enough the rest of the class had joined in, taunting me while I stared at them all, horrified that they did not understand me. Laughter and ghost noises continued to come from all sides, until all I could feel was the burn of saltwater in my eyes.

I really don't intend to portray myself as a victim. I am trying to remember my early experiences as they happened to me, reliving those moments, turning them over in my mind until I can see them clearly, trying to understand how I came to be so alone and so sure that I would always feel this way. I cannot understand who I am today without knowing who I was before. This is not to say that my childhood was all suffering and no joy; I had a roof over my head, a warm bed at night and a couple of close friends; I went to the beach during the holidays; my father took me to Paris when I was eight, where I drank my first black coffee and spat it out all over the white rug in the apartment; I went to the funfair and had a pet cat named Zazie who used to lie next to my head and purr in my ear until I fell asleep. There were many things that made life much sweeter, but there were also details I would prefer to erase. I spent many years trying to do so, but recently certain memories have been coming back.

The first instance of this was about a month ago, before I met Val. I had been living in Paris for two and a half years, and since moving here I had grown increasingly lonely; perhaps it's the indifference of this vast and sprawling city, and all the unmet expectations I had about my life here. I'd made a conscious effort not to think about my father since leaving England. I wanted a clean slate, where I could be Marie the writer, Marie the filmmaker, Marie the muse — not the forgettable silhouette of a girl I had been my whole life. Two and a half years later, and nothing had changed in that regard. I had become deeply depressed, to the point where my sadness embarrassed me; I didn't want anyone to know that the gap between who I was and where I wanted to be had expanded into an abyss.

On this particular night I'd been lying awake long into the early hours, my head rotating the same set of thoughts like a conveyor belt until I couldn't bear it any longer and fell asleep. The next thing I knew I was back in the graveyard in Oxfordshire with my father. I was five years old again, as if no time had passed. I could hear the click of his thumbs on the tape recorder, and the rustling of wind in the trees. Everything played out exactly as I remembered it, only somehow more vividly, as if someone had edited this memory together into a perfectly cut film for my own private viewing. At first I tried not to look at the church, keeping my eyes fixed on the ground, the tangled grass curling around my ankles in the warm breeze. I could feel the sun's heat on my neck, burning into my skin as I grew simultaneously hot and cold — hot on the outside and cold within, as if there were a magnetic weight in the pit of my stomach, smooth and cool and perfectly round. I could see him standing in the threshold of the church, his hat a faint outline against the dim archway.

My father was imploring me to speak — *say hello, Marie* — as he had before, but in the dream I found myself unable to speak. I hadn't simply returned to my younger body, but was trapped in it, confined to the movements of my child self, as the Tall Man stepped into the light. Around six and a half foot, he wore a long black coat and a brimmed hat which obscured his face like a character from a film noir, his shadow weighing over him. All I could feel was a numb kind of terror.

It was as if I were looking back on this moment in my past, knowing it could not be undone.

I woke up at that point. The graveyard was gone, and I was back in my bedroom in Paris. Everything was normal; the film posters were still tacked to the walls, my books still lined the shelves, and the thin white curtains were drawn, diffusing the light from outside. I remember looking down at my own body, and it was once again the twenty-one-year-old self I had left behind when I shut my eyes. I sat up in bed, feeling disoriented yet strangely well-rested.

I got up to open the curtains. The sunlit Rue de Bagnolet lay before me — a beautiful day. I love the light in this city; it has a reflective quality, bouncing off the wall of one building and landing on the next, forever chasing itself. This is not a place built for darkness, but for an abundance of light. I opened the window wide, allowing myself to become consumed by Paris, placing my hands on the sill and breathing in the scent of tarmac mixed with fresh leaves and exhaust fumes, the rev of a scooter engine with the trill of a bicycle bell and a man's voice from a street corner. I closed my eyes and leaned further out of the window; I have often contemplated what it would feel like if I were to slip over the edge of time…

A loud chiming pulled me back inside — my phone alarm. I turned and caught myself in the mirror, my bobbed hair curving gently above my shoulders, thick bangs on either side, my eyes tired as usual. I went to switch my alarm off, and was reminded that it was the 18th May.

I got dressed, went into the kitchen and — as Anna and I had spontaneously decided the night before — began making crêpes with the eggs I had in the cupboard.

'Morning!' Anna's shrill voice came from behind me.

She was leaning against the doorway, wearing a dark blue summer dress with small daises printed on it.

'Morning!' I replied, sounding far more lively than I expected to.

Anna made coffee as I fried the crêpes. There was a certain lightness to the morning, with the coffee, the jar of fresh marigolds on the windowsill, and Françoise Hardy's *Tous les garçons et les filles* drifting from the record player.

I focused on frying the crêpes and listening to the music, carefully translating the lyrics in my head:

> *All the boys and the girls of my age*
> *They walk down the street two by two*
> *All the boys and the girls of my age*
> *Know well what it is to be happy*
>
> *Eyes in eyes*
> *And hand in hand*
> *They fall in love*
> *Without fear of tomorrow*
>
> *Yes, but I, I go alone*
> *In the streets, the lost soul*
> *Yes, but I, I am alone*
> *Because nobody loves me...*

As I listened to the cyclical playground-melody of *Tous les garçons*, my mind was pulled back in the direction of my dream. Did it hark back to a real memory at all, or had the Tall Man always belonged to the realm of nightmares? It was all so long ago now, and it's not uncommon for children to conflate their dreams with reality. It was quite possible that I had never seen this man in my waking life at all.

The crêpe in the pan had turned a rich golden colour, and it occurred to me that I had just spent the past five minutes functioning on autopilot, unable to remember if I had sliced up those lemons on the counter, or if Anna had done that. Had I taken the sugar out of the cupboard and put it on the table, or had she? My mind felt incredibly hazy. I passed the plate with the crêpe to Anna, hearing myself say *voilà* triumphantly. She complimented my cooking, and asked why she couldn't ever get her crêpes to taste this good. I laughed awkwardly, telling her I would burn the next one. I tried to snap out of whatever this dissociative feeling was as I turned back to the stove and ladled some more batter into the pan.

'Did you ever hear back from Olivier?' Anna asked casually.

That was enough to drag me straight back into the present. Olivier was just one of the many young men I had met here, who had essentially decided I was not what they were looking for. He was nothing to me, if not one more link in a chain of romantic disappointments. I looked up at Anna and feigned indifference.

'I gave up waiting.'

'*Seriously?*' she said, more exasperated than I could ever admit to being. I felt myself rapidly deflating.

'It's fine. It was just a couple of dates.'

'Even so, is it so much to ask to get back to someone?'

I tried to tell her it didn't matter, but she didn't believe me.

'It doesn't!' I persisted. Suddenly I didn't feel detached from reality at all anymore, but very much stuck in it, as if there were an invisible dome preventing me from leaving this conversation. Eventually Anna wore me down with an intense stare and I gave in, admitting that I did care after all.

'But what can I do about it?' I said.

'You can opt out of dating, you know. Why don't we go and see a film later? It will get your mind off things.'

I nodded; it wasn't such a bad idea.

Suddenly, Anna yelped.

'Marie!' she said, leaping up, her eyes fixed on the stove. I spun around, and realised what she was panicking about; a small plume of smoke was rising from the pan with a blackened crêpe inside. Anna grabbed a tea towel and I turned off the heat. We fell about laughing.

'I told you I would burn it.'

After breakfast, we cycled through the springtime streets, the warm weather saturating everything in a haze of nostalgia for future days; if I close my eyes now I can find myself back in those narrow streets, followed by the sunbaked walls of the Père Lachaise; then arriving in the 11th arrondissement, seeing the chic twenty-somethings smoking outside cafés; the girl selling flowers by the Tabac; the teenagers on the street corner. There had been a dreamlike feeling in the air that morning, something unreal about the city that had made this day stand out from the others. We had gone into the Tabac and bought our Gauloises, and I left with a lightness in my step, which remained there until we arrived at the university. In all my confusion that morning, I had managed to forget once again that I had a presentation to deliver. Today I was going to be pitching *Sacred Hearts*.

I felt tense the moment I entered the classroom. It is a plain, sparse room, the kind of place that is cold even in summer. A few vintage film posters — *Blow-Up, À Bout de Souffle, The Graduate* — spruce up the otherwise bare walls. I would not be surprised if the place hadn't been redecorated since 1967. I also have a strange feeling that all the film students in this room preferred it that way. It shielded us from the harsh reality of the film world; a fast-moving, overwhelming place in which movies are products, not comments on capitalism or the postmodern condition; a world in which writing a script is not a vocation, but a ninety-page attempt to grab a producer's attention. I have lived under the illusion of film school for the past two and a half years, only because I do not want to fall out of love with cinema.

Anna did her pitch before me. She stood at the front of the class with her shoulders back, notably poised and confident.

'More than anything I want this film to provide a woman's perspective on what it means to be looked at,' she said. 'In subverting the romance genre, *Vanity* will question how we see women in cinema, and more importantly, how they see themselves.'

She was coming to the end of her presentation. She surveyed the room, finished. The class applauded her pitch. Professor Herbaut delivered his feedback.

'Very good, Anna. I think it's a timely concept, putting us in the position of the woman-being-looked-at.'

Anna nodded and smiled broadly.

'But I do have to say, I was left wondering what your pitch *adds* to the feminist discussion. While I can see how your film might explore the impact of the male gaze from a woman's perspective, what else are you bringing to the table that say, a Sofia Coppola or Agnès Varda film hasn't already?'

There was a palpable ripple of suspense throughout the room. I suddenly felt very bad for Anna; I'd seen how diligently she'd worked on her pitch over the past couple of weeks, and it hardly seemed fair that she'd immediately been challenged on it. The smile was wiped from her face. She looked embarrassed.

'By all means it's a good start,' Herbaut continued, 'but my gut instinct is that you need to go deeper — to become more intimately involved in the story you're telling, to truly make it your own.'

Of course, what Professor Herbaut was saying was every bit true, but I couldn't help but empathise with Anna. To be critiqued on one's writerly technique was one thing, but to be accused of lacking originality was another. Anna nodded meekly, forcing a gracious smile.

I was up next. Ever since that fateful show-and-tell incident, I have never felt comfortable with public speaking. I felt a lump forming in my throat as my name was called, and knew that people would be able to hear it when I spoke, that my voice would tremble and falter. I could feel my face sinking, and quickly masked it with a smile.

'So, Marie,' Herbaut prompted me, 'tell us about your idea.'

'Well…' I began, hearing my own voice exactly as I expected it to sound: weak. I carried on in spite of myself. '*Sacred Hearts* is about a young woman who decides that falling in love will cure her loneliness.'

I paused, only to be confronted with a wall of silence and blank stares. I continued.

'The protagonist, Elizabeth, moves to Paris in the hope of meeting her soulmate. She's always believed that she will find love in the city, because of all the films she's watched. As time has gone on, she's realised that life is nothing like a film.'

I stopped speaking. My attention was immediately drawn to a student whispering something at the back of the class. I tried to ignore it, to continue:

'So…I wanted to tell this story because sometimes…'

The whispering seemed to grow louder.

'…sometimes loneliness is…'

It grew louder still, more intense — sinister, even. It was not coming from my classmates anymore, but from all around me. It was building into an intolerable sound, until I stopped speaking entirely, and was unable to move my lips. All I could think of was being back in that classroom many years ago, attacked by mock ghost noises and laughter. For all the years that had passed, I felt exactly the same.

I pulled myself out of this memory and back into the room, in which the whispering had now been replaced by a hung silence. All eyes were on me.

'Thank you, Marie,' Professor Herbaut's voice suddenly came from my right hand side.

I had forgotten that he was even there. Anna was looking around at the other students, the subtlest hint of a smile upon her face. I didn't know what she was smiling at, but I wished she wasn't. Herbaut had little to say about my pitch, instead emphasising that we should break for lunch.

I told Anna I would meet her outside, hoping that we would somehow miss each other, and I would be able to spend the break reading my book. I went out onto the college green and planted myself under the old oak tree, leaning my back against its trunk as if it might swallow me up, with any luck.

I hadn't got so far as opening my book, when I heard Anna call my name. She was striding towards me with purpose.

'Marie, are you okay?' she said, sitting down beside me. I told her I was, not wanting to start a conversation about it.

'Are you sure?' she persisted. 'You seemed a bit upset in class.'

I told her that I just didn't like presenting.

'Me either,' she replied.

'But you did great.'

My response fell very flat, and we both knew it. I wondered if it was possible to lack talent, or if it was more simply a matter of finding one's niche. I liked to believe it was the latter, if only for my own sake. I knew I was not remarkable by nature.

'It was brave of you to stand up there and talk about something so… *personal*,' Anna said, but instead of hearing a compliment, I couldn't ignore the condescension with which she imbued the word 'personal.' I don't understand why it is a mark of courage to tell one's own story. Surely that's the only story we are truly qualified to tell. Her eyes fell to my copy of *Good Morning, Midnight* on the grass, and for a moment she looked as if she was about to say something — and then she didn't.

That's when I saw him. He was walking across the grass with a book nestled under his arm; a tall, young man with dark brown hair that hung wildly around his face; the kind of face that makes people desirous of a more poetic life. There are certain people you cannot imagine doing something as banal as hanging up the washing or paying their phone bill without it becoming an act of creativity; I was always drawn to such people.

He waved at Anna. His smile was unexpectedly warm, a flash of fire across the grass, igniting something within myself. I wished for a moment that I was not so easily possessed by my desires.

'Who's that?' I said.

'That's Val. He's in my cinematography class.'

He passed by and I pretended not to care.

'He's your type,' Anna remarked, seeing right through my nonchalant non-glances. 'He probably sleeps around,' she added drily.

'What makes you say that?' I was surprised at how defensive I sounded, as if I had any idea.

'He's too good-looking, so he's probably aware of it. He's probably got six different girls he's stringing along right now,' Anna stated, as if this were supremely obvious.

'Isn't that quite a cynical way to look at things?' I replied.

'I'm not being *cynical*,' she responded, 'I'm just telling you, this is what men are like when they know they're good-looking. They exploit it.'

Anna paused, as I began to pluck a blade of grass out of the ground and twist it around my little finger, very tightly.

'I don't know,' she continued, 'I just think maybe you should consider dating outside your type…'

Anna always brought this up at some point or other. She wasn't necessarily wrong, but I couldn't help who I was attracted to. On the face of things this was a piece of practical advice, but after some examination it always unravelled itself to reveal a deeper criticism of my hopes. I rested my head on my knees and looked up at the sky. The breeze was rustling gently through the trees, and the birds were singing. I could stay here forever, I thought, drinking up the light, the warmth.

That evening I went to the cinema alone. Anna had cancelled because her boyfriend, Luc, said he had some important news to share with her. I went to see *Le Rayon Vert* which was playing at Le Voile, the old art deco cinema on Rue La Fayette. It is the same cinema I had once visited with my father to watch *Les Quatre Cents Coups* when I was eight years old. At the time I had not understood the story, but it nonetheless ignited a love of film which had embedded itself under my skin and quite possibly brought me here today. The red curtains and dim lights of the cinema have always been seductive to me, evoking a past both unreal yet familiar; a time of silk dresses and starlets, of reels of film being unwound by the dusty light of a projector, of young couples who came here because there was nothing on TV, who rested their heads on each other's shoulders and kissed quietly in the darkness.

After the film, I stood in the lobby and thought about buying a drink. My attention was soon drawn to a man stood by the door, chatting to a woman. I recognised him, but I didn't know where from. He was possibly in his late forties, good-looking and well-groomed, perhaps even semi-famous, which would explain why he looked so familiar. Before I had time to ponder the matter further, I was distracted by my phone vibrating. It was a call from an unknown UK number. I hesitated for a moment, my thumb hovering over the answer button. Surely not, I told myself, surely not. I dismissed the thought, and answered the phone.

'Hello?' I said, keeping my voice low.

'Marie?' my father's voice rang out.

In an instant my whole body became tense. My eyes had made their way back up to the silver-haired man by the door, purely as something to anchor themselves to.

'Marie, is that you?' he repeated.

'It's me,' I confirmed. I was shocked by how flat my voice sounded. I sank down into a chair and stared at the floor.

'Marie, it's Dad.'

I didn't reply at first; I didn't do anything. I was unable to move any part of my body; my eyes remained fixed on the black and white squares of marble laid out like a chessboard beneath my feet.

'How did you get my number?' I asked him.

'I got in touch with your college and asked for it. I told them I was your dad, of course,' he said with a chuckle, as if it were some kind of joke.

'I told you not to call me.'

It went very quiet on the other end of the line. I waited, unsure of what to do next; but then he sobbed, loud and mournful, his breath slicing the air between the phone and my ear. I was just on the verge of hanging up when my nerve failed me.

'Are you okay?' I said. The square tiles at my feet seemed to shift as I gazed at them, as if the world were somehow more fluid and volatile than I understood it to be.

'Do you remember what day it is?' he asked me. The sounds of the lobby paled into oblivion, and all I could do was stare at the the shifting squares beneath my feet. Did I remember? How does a person ever forget the day that their mother drove a car off a viaduct, and the night that they screamed in their cot, stomach growling as the surviving parent drank themselves to a point of sickness? People do not forget days like that, even if they do not consciously remember it; days like that stay in the body, regenerating into our cells.

'You have no right to call me about this,' I replied.

'Marie—'

'Please stop.'

I hung up and stormed out of the cinema, furious that my day had been disrupted not once, but twice by the memory of what should have been gone and buried by now, entombed beneath six feet of cold, black soil. On my way out, I encountered a young man who told me to smile, and found myself using every ounce of willpower to resist pushing him into the oncoming traffic. I continued down the neon-lit street, where car motors revved, and horns beeped in the distance, light pollution filling the sky. My pace quickened, the bustle of the city suddenly overwhelming. I walked for I don't know how long, until I found myself in some forgotten *banlieue*, huge tower blocks to my right and a wire fence to my left. It was eerily dark, but I was not afraid of walking late at night here; to me this was just a huge urban wasteland, where nothing more could hurt me. I stopped and listened. The city sounds were now more distant, the world far less crowded.

I continued again, the sound of my footsteps the only sign of life around me. After a few more minutes of walking, I came to a closed off road; and there it was, about thirty feet ahead of me, the huge, derelict viaduct where my mother had taken her life. I ignored the concrete blockades in front of it, proceeding along the bridge. Weeds tangled up through the cracked tarmac, rising and wilting in one movement. The bridge itself was high, frightening and dusky, the sky stretching out into a thick gauze of nothingness. The drop beneath me was formidable, and what was once a river was now a dilapidated trench, the terrain scattered with dried up shrubbery, rocks and dead grass. I don't know exactly how I found my way there that night; I had not set foot there since I was eight, when my father had taken me to Paris.

I had no desire to remember what had happened the last time I visited the viaduct. I have spent a long time trying to forget, and to become the woman I am today. I have tried not to hear the song that was on the radio the day my father drove us through the *banlieues*; I have tried not to feel the warm sunlight on my cheeks; I have tried to wipe away the stoic expression on his face as he ignored my attempts at conversation, and turned down the music as we neared the bridge; I have tried not to see the rundown tower blocks and empty construction sites around us.

I just need to drop something off, he'd said. It's what he always said whenever we went for a drive. He was either dropping something off or picking something up, always leaving and returning empty-handed, to the point that I wondered what he was hiding. I never got to the bottom of it; it seemed he simply wanted to drive around with me in the passenger seat, always insisting that I come with him to fulfil this elusive, never-ending errand. At the time I thought nothing of his typical excuse until he pulled up on top of the bridge — a strange place to deliver or receive something. As usual, he told me to wait in the car.

Why? I quizzed him this time. What could he possibly have to drop off at this high and lonely place?

I'm just dropping something off, he repeated. *Promise you'll wait in the car, okay?*

I complied, albeit frustrated that I was not allowed to know where he was going. He took a deep breath and opened the car door; the warm spring air rushed in, smothering me in a blanket of dense heat. He got out and slammed the door behind him. In the wing mirror I watched him take a bouquet of flowers from the boot of the car and descend to the river. A knot formed in the pit of my stomach, as I suddenly realised where we might be. The clock on the dashboard read 1.55pm. It occurred to me that perhaps if I closed my eyes for long enough, I could fall asleep, and when I woke up we would be back at the apartment my father had rented in the 11th arrondissement. I attempted to do just that, but when I opened my eyes again it was 2.17pm and my father had still not returned from his errand. I looked out of the window, and could just make out the river beneath me — but no sign of my father. My cheeks were hot and flushed, and my entire head felt numb, the excruciating sun beating in through the windows with no fresh air at all. I pulled back on the door handle and swung my feet out, miscalculating where the ground was and falling straight onto the tarmac, grazing my hands as they met the shards of gravel beneath them.

Fingers bleeding, I made my way down to the river. There was a long, narrow stairway leading to the bottom of the viaduct, nothing short of a descent to Hell, where the sun was eternally scorching and there was nothing but a rancid pool of life's leftovers beneath me. I was about halfway down the steps when I saw him. He was standing in the water, the bouquet of flowers floating beside him. He had his back to me and appeared to be talking to someone. I crept down, trying to make out what he was saying. When I got to the riverbank, I realised that he was hysterical.

Fuck! Why! Julie, why did you do this to me!

He was kicking the water frantically, as I watched him ask the same question over and over again, begging to know why his wife and my mother had done such a terrible thing. *Why is the only question worth asking*. These words rang in my ears as a death knell; if why was really the only question worth asking, then surely we must resign ourselves to a world without answers. He buried his head in his hands and cried as I edged closer.

Why, why, why! he continued, possessed by a grief so monstrous it caused his voice to break each time he yelled out to the brown water which stagnated around his ankles. There was no glimpse of hope in that moment. There was nothing in the way my father bent down to retrieve the bouquet of flowers, that suggested any kind of tenderness; or in the way he hugged them close to his chest to imply that I was loved, or cared for by this man. He cared more about a bunch of drowned flowers than he did about me. He whispered something to them, stroking them, and I could see that he had entered into another realm, off the map, somewhere far beyond the world that I knew. I couldn't take it anymore and burst into tears. My father stopped everything and turned around. We stared at each other, speechless, for an unquantifiable amount of time, but it was long enough for me to understand that this man was not — and could never be — my father.

Standing on the same bridge thirteen years later, a vague feeling of terror arose; it was the same sensation from my dream, as if the world around me could dissolve at any second, the curtain drawn up to reveal an impenetrable darkness. It was almost impossible to feel any kind of connection to time and place, especially as I found myself pulling my phone out of my pocket, turning it over in my fingers like some foreign object, ignoring the three missed calls I had from Anna. I once read that when people stand at a great height, they no longer envision throwing themselves off the precipice, but their phones. I think this is because the phone has become a vessel for our thoughts, for unwanted reminders and knowledge that overwhelms us. The sudden urge to just drop all of that into the abyss is a new form of suicide; it is the desire to become free from these intrusive projections of ourselves. With surprising ease, I let my phone slip free from my fingers, and watched it fall into the trench below, until the slim black body was swallowed up by the night.

I cried on the Métro home, and when I glanced at the window I was met with my reflection, pale and haggard under the anaemic light. I was repelled by it. As the train pulled into Avron station, I watched the passengers file out; the hordes of Friday night partygoers; the evening commuters; bar workers on their way to the night shift. Then, I froze in my seat. Among the interweaving passengers, I saw a figure I couldn't ignore. He was dressed in a long black coat and a trilby hat, his face hidden behind the other commuters. I had forgotten to breathe, not daring to look away until he had walked across the platform and was out of sight, never once revealing his face. Instantly I remembered my dream, and understood that this was no coincidence — especially not on a night like this. I was jolted back into the present by a group of drunk people boarding the train and talking loudly. I sunk back into my seat and let the abrasive sound of their chatter swell around me.

When I got home, there was loud music and several voices coming from inside the apartment. I reread the number on the front door, double checking that I hadn't walked to the wrong floor. I realised that perhaps if I hadn't thrown my phone off a bridge I would have some vague idea of what was going on. I opened the door and found myself in a smoke-filled apartment, music pounding from the next room, where blue and red lights flashed into the hallway. There were perhaps thirty people in the living room, who were dancing, smoking, kissing in dark corners and conversing on the sofa; Anna and Luc were embracing by the speakers; in the centre of the room, people were dancing under a large disco ball; by the window, Val was lighting a cigarette. My breath got caught in my throat. Noticing me, Anna came over, her eyes wide with excitement and most likely something stronger. She gave me a generous hug, kissing me on both cheeks.

'Marie! Where have you been?'

'What's going on?!' I asked, bewildered; Anna was not one to throw impromptu gatherings, especially not ones of twenty-five to thirty people, some of whom I had never seen before in my life. I wondered how she had got Val to come. She put her arm around my shoulder, and proceeded to explain.

'I'm so sorry I didn't tell you sooner! I tried to call, but you weren't picking up.' I gazed around, completely lost.

'It's okay,' I replied, 'it's just…'

'Luc's got great news,' she interjected. 'We had to celebrate!'

'What is it?'

'Luc!' Anna summoned him from a few inches behind her. Luc turned his head towards me and casually glanced over my shoulder, as if nothing could be so exciting as to ruffle his perpetual stoicism. I had always thought they were an odd pairing, with Anna's predilection to small talk, and Luc's refusal to say anything that wasn't absolutely necessary to progress a conversation. She put both arms around him, and he smiled in a way that suggested he was high on something too.

'Luc got a job in New York!' Anna gushed. I was genuinely surprised. It seemed very sudden for someone who had never mentioned such a thing before; but that was not inconceivable for Luc. My mouth hung open stupidly.

'Oh my God — congratulations!'

'I'm so proud of you,' Anna said, turning to Luc, looking adoringly into his eyes.

'That's really great news!' I said.

'It's exciting,' came the monotone reply from Luc. He took a long sip of beer and glanced around the room, looking for a way to extricate himself from the conversation. I looked around too, stunned at the party taking place in my living room — which admittedly I might have known about if I still had my phone. Anna led me to the fridge where she had stored a few beers on my behalf. She handed me a cold bottle of Kronenbourg and shot me a playful glance.

'I got Val to come,' she said with a smile. This gave me permission to look at Val again, who was still standing by the window. He noticed and momentarily returned my gaze, before we both quickly looked away. To him, I was probably just another girl in another smoke-filled apartment. But to me, Val was the embodiment of all that was inaccessible in this world. Anna smiled at me, and I couldn't help but smile back.

'I thought you said he was bad news,' I reminded her.

'Maybe,' she sighed, 'but…then I thought about it, and then I thought about you, and I realised, it would be fun to invite him. Besides, it's not like you have any other prospects.'

That hurt more than I wanted it to. It was such a weighted comment that I wasn't entirely convinced Anna didn't know it. I tried to laugh it off, but my chuckles drifted out uneasily.

'Oh, I didn't mean it like *that*,' Anna said. 'I just mean you don't have anyone else on your radar.'

Of course she did. I forced myself to smile. Anna grinned back and I remembered that she was high, she wasn't thinking about everything she was saying; that much was obvious from the way she was biting her lip and clearly having an unspeakably good time.

'What are you on?' I said.

'Oh — Luc and I got some pills. Do you want one?' I thought about it. Everything inside me felt so broken, I could have done with a pick-me-up. But I knew it was a bad idea. In fact, what I wanted to do was to go straight to bed and cry every last teardrop out of me, until my pillow resembled a white sponge.

'I shouldn't,' I said.

'Why not?'

'I've got some things to do tomorrow and...'

Anna continued to stare at me.

'Have you been crying?'

I wiped the debris of my makeup from under my eyes.

'Oh—no. This eyeliner! It smudges everywhere.'

The rest of the party was a blur. I made some excuse I don't remember to get out of there, and within ten minutes I was on my bike, cycling through the night past garishly lit corner shops and graffitied walls, everything dissolving by in a wash of colour. I didn't know where I was going.

I must have cycled for at least twenty-five minutes, because I ended up in Montmartre, suddenly finding myself passing quaint bars on cobblestone streets. I parked my bike at the bottom of Square Louise-Michel, and noticed on the wall above it a poster for *Ville de Nuit: A film by Jacques Beaudet.* The poster depicted a 1960s-style drawing —

like the vintage film posters that are plastered around our classroom — of a young woman, with the same haircut as me. She was stood atop a high balcony, over a sea of sprawling buildings, lit up like hundreds of minuscule lanterns. I couldn't take my eyes off it. The name *Jacques Beaudet* rang a bell — albeit one that I couldn't place. There was something strange about this poster. I turned and looked up at the Sacré-Coeur, glowing white against the sky, and ascended the steps towards it.

When I got to the top, I was met with a soft breeze and the sound of distant traffic. I sat on the parapet outside the basilica, where the buildings beyond were glowing gold and orange, sprawling out onto the horizon until they were faint, blurry dots. It was very quiet and I could feel the breeze running through my hair. I cannot say what led me to that place, or what exactly I was looking for in that moment. If anything, I needed a sign that someone was looking out for me. Not in the sense that Anna was looking out for me, but in the more metaphysical sense. Long before I met Anna I had lived with certain memories that no friend, however close, could possibly understand. Ever since I had come to Paris, I'd longed for somebody to help me carry the burden of being here. But there was no one. I just needed a sign.

Then it happened. The clock struck twelve, the bells ringing out across the city, an almost reproachful sound, each knell flung back against itself like a macabre yo-yo. Why should such a sacred place produce such gloomy sounds? My body seemed to lose its weight, and like the echoes of the bells became part of the darkness, until I felt myself suspended in the air, about to fall to certain death. At that precise moment, a hand gripped my wrist, preventing me from going any further.

'*Stop!*' a man's voice implored, ringing with panic. I turned to look at my saviour, and was stunned to see Val's eyes staring into mine; eyes wide with fear. I blinked and he was still there, his hand clenching my wrist.

'Are you okay?' he said. I couldn't look away from where Val's fingers met my flesh. I didn't know what had happened. He had been lighting a cigarette in my living room less than an hour ago; I didn't understand.

'Are you hurt?' he said, as if his presence didn't require an explanation, as if it all made perfect sense that he should be here at this moment, and now we could go home and talk calmly and drink tea and balance would be restored.

Up close he was even more attractive, his eyes a deep brown, his skin a pale shade of olive, nose perfectly shaped; but it was his lips I found my eyes returning to; they were the loveliest pair I had ever seen, and to kiss them, I thought, would be bliss. I reprimanded myself for thinking such stupid thoughts while this was all happening. Val escorted me away from the ledge and we sat down on the steps a little way back from the parapet.

'What happened?' he asked.

It was a loaded question and I didn't know where to begin. The warmth of his body next to mine was palpable, and suddenly Val had shifted into a real human presence, not the romantic mirage who had sauntered across the grass that afternoon, which was now faded in my memory like an old photograph, its edges softened by the sun and time passing. I still had not said a word. He must have been beginning to wonder if I was unable to speak. His brow furrowed, thinking of what else to say, to justify his coming here and intercepting my fall.

'What's your name?' he eventually asked.

'Marie,' I replied, very slowly, hesitant.

'Marie. Okay. I'm…my name's Val.'

I know, I wanted to say. *I haven't stopped noticing you all day.* Instead I just sat there shaking, the cool night suddenly freezing, with Val's presence sinking deeper beneath my skin as we became unified by this strange moment.

'Are you cold?' he said, taking off his jacket and draping it over my shoulders. It was irresistibly comfortable, and as I pulled it over my body I could feel his eyes resting on me, evaluating how I looked in his jacket. It crossed my mind that if Val hadn't been so attractive, I might have been more disturbed — perhaps even frightened — that he was here at all.

'You followed me here,' I said. I wanted to hear what he had to say, turning over in my mind the idea that he had been *compelled* to follow me.

'I'm sorry…' he replied, almost sheepishly. 'I saw you looked upset, so I got on my bike…I don't know what came over me…but I didn't trust where you were going. I'm sorry, in hindsight I shouldn't have assumed…' he trailed off, his eyes falling to the floor.

'If you hadn't been around to save me just now, I would have died,' I said. I was still stumped, and the truism that everything happens for a reason suddenly hit me with full force.

'I suppose it must have been fate,' Val said.

There was a soft glimmer in his eye as he said it, and I found myself struggling to hold his gaze. I decided that Val must be short for Valentin, a name which took you to rose gardens with old stone paths and black coffee served in ceramic mugs, or a promontory scattered with wildflowers where you could lie down in the grass and laugh at the clouds together, the scent of the earth lingering under summer skies.

'And you believe in fate?' I asked him; and he gave the only honest reply there is:

'What choice do I have?'

I returned my gaze to the skyline, to the gleaming ocean of lights stretching out to the very edges of the city.

'I should go home,' I said.

'Yeah. I'm sorry. I just wanted to know if you were okay.'

'It's okay. I should get going.'

'Sure. I should probably get home too.'

Val proceeded to walk me down the hill. We walked in total silence. When we reached the bottom, I returned his jacket and unlocked my bike, suddenly feeling I was unable to look at him. I felt we would never meet again. Mounting my bike, I turned to Val and smiled, remembering his face.

'Do you want me to cycle you home?' he said.

'I'll be okay. Thank you though.'

I couldn't bring myself to tell him that of course I wanted him to cycle me home, more than anything. About halfway up the street though, my legs gave up pedalling. I slowed to a halt and turned around. Val was stood a few yards behind me with his bike. It had just started to rain; a warm, spring rain — the kind that leaves you both full and empty at once.

'Come home with me,' I said.

When we got back, we were drenched. The party was still going, but we slipped past and went straight into my room. My hair was wet, and so was his. By the time I had shut the curtains to block out the street, he was stood right next to me; not touching me, but his body emanating closeness. A second later, our lips brushed together as he took me in his arms and began to kiss me; at first gently — perhaps even cautiously. But it wasn't long before we grew more passionate, and soon enough we were gripping each other tightly as I slid my tongue over his and the room began to fall away.

I was surprised, when he lay me down on the bed, at the tenderness of his mouth on my skin, its warmth and softness as he kissed each part of my body, and felt the wetness between my legs with his fingers. When he finally entered me, I decided I would want nothing else in the world ever again.

***

Things progressed with Val very quickly, but in a way that made up for all the time I had wasted being heartbroken over men who were never serious about me anyway. We bonded over our love of cinema, and I told him about how my mother was an actress who had worked with Rohmer in the eighties.

'Your mother is French?' Val asked, perhaps surprised that I hadn't mentioned it sooner.

'She was,' I said. He didn't ask any more questions about her; he must have felt uncomfortable with the idea that she was no longer alive.

'Have you ever noticed how in New Wave films everybody has a gun?' he asked, changing the subject.

'It's true!' I replied, smiling.

'Even in the romance stories, Jean-Pierre Léaud still manages to pull out a revolver while he's on a date.' I laughed, not just because it was funny, but because my heart felt soft and light.

There was no spoken agreement between us, but Val and I worked in tandem to transform our own lives into a *nouvelle vague* film. Nothing we did changed drastically or was particularly unusual; it was just the way we approached them. Whether it was lying in the park or travelling on the Métro, I found myself no longer caring about things which would previously have troubled me. I began to rejoice in simple things, like noticing the smell of the rain on the leaves, and the different shades of the sky throughout the day. I began to realise how impermanent everything was, and how the dark clouds that hunched over the city like vultures would always disperse at some point. And rather than feeling like I was becoming someone else, it was more like uncovering a long-lost part of myself, an inner sense of connectedness to the world around me. I didn't need to ask if this was happiness. As long as I remained in this state, there were no more questions to be asked.

Part II

II

The women in the hairdressers are all very beautiful under the warm light, reflected in the mirrors. I am having my hair trimmed to its usual length, skimming the shoulders, with long bangs just touching my eyebrows. I do think it is important for a person to feel beautiful. And I do wonder sometimes, where I would be in this world if my hair were that bit softer, my eyes a drop bluer, my skin a touch smoother. My trips to the hairdressers always make me feel that bit closer to this ideal version of myself.

'*C'est bon?*' the hairdresser says, holding his scissors just under my hair.

'*Oui, génial,*' I reply, as he pulls the scissors away and my hair falls more naturally onto my shoulders.

'I do think,' the hairdresser says, 'you would suit a shorter bob as well, you know; you are very chic, in fact it might make you look *too* chic for your own good.'

I cannot tell whether he is after a generous tip or paying me a genuine compliment. I suppose in a world where a compliment is a form of payment, I must give him something in return. I blush and smile.

'Unquestionably,' replies the hairdresser attending to the woman next to me. 'You always look so good; and you cannot buy style.' I don't know what to say.

'Thank you,' the words issue quietly from my mouth; I must sound so smug, I think, *thank you, thank you, thank you,* as if the world were offering me a bouquet of roses.

As I leave the hairdressers, I catch my reflection in the window and almost don't recognise myself. I can't help but notice how love seems to severed a before from an after — it was almost as if I were two different people: Marie before Val, and Marie with Val. I think about how the French for *before* and *with* are similar; *avant* and *avec* — as if one should precede the other.

I look at the time and it is half past five; in three hours I will be drinking a cocktail with Anna at a bar in Oberkampf. I walk along the Avenue Gambetta, looking up at the trees, that are patched with sunlight. The evening shadows have just begun to creep along the branches, inching slowly towards the bright leaves at the ends. Reaching the Gambetta roundabout, I feel myself being watched by the middle-aged man with wrinkled skin in the red Citroën. I make very brief eye contact, but he doesn't look away. I pretend not to have been staring at him right in the face a half-second before, and quickly pass the car.

Down the next street there is the right wing of the town hall. I stop outside, and look up at the cream stone walls, the pink flowers on the windowsills, and I wonder what it must be like to live in a grand old house. Little by little, questions begin to arise in my mind. What shall I do when I leave university? I am studying film, but what for? On my way home I listen out for conversations that might contain some shred of an answer.

'*Il fait un peu frais!*' a man says to a woman as they walk past.

On my way home I make a detour to the Père Lachaise to catch the last of the day's sunlight, and perhaps read a little; but by the time I get to the cemetery I can feel the air cooling. The sunburnt leaves dance across the cobbled paths lined with tombs and headstones. I decide to stay anyway, to finish what is left of *Good Morning, Midnight*. The novel is about a woman living in Paris between the two World Wars, trapped between the life she is fleeing and the one she is trying to forge. I am fascinated by the book, not only because I can relate to the story, but because of how unsuccessful it was upon publication — sales dwindled quickly, and critics thought the novel far too depressing, despite its literary merit. This gave me some obscure hope for my own stories — that even if I fail in this life, there might always be some pining academic who discovers an old screenplay or rough cut in fifty years' time, and sees something in it. Perhaps it is narcissistic to say such a thing, but an artist has to believe their work will matter to someone, or it may as well remain an idea.

I am reading the novel when I feel something at my side. I look up, as the shadows of the trees recede into a less threatening vignette. There is no one beside me. I look around the empty graveyard for signs of life. I think I find one; but as I peer closer at the figure in the distance, I feel myself recoiling — the black coat and the trilby hat are half-concealed behind an ash tree. He is watching me. I slam my book shut and run as fast as I can.

It is seven-thirty by the time I get home. I lean my back against the door, breathing heavily as the world grows narrower and I can't get his figure out of my mind, his face hidden beneath an opaque shadow, his gaze direct and impenetrable.

'Where have you been?'

I jump out of my skin. It's Anna's voice, calling from the next room. I poke my head around the corner to find her sitting on the sofa, reading a magazine. A glass of red wine sits next to a half-empty bottle on the coffee table. She raises her eyebrows, awaiting my response.

'I was getting my hair cut,' I say, touching the bottom of my hair where it now curves inwards, like a 1960s mannequin. Anna looks somewhat exasperated.

'You weren't seeing Val?' The way she asks it is odd and accusatory.

'No, why?'

I can tell she is drunk by the way her eyes are struggling to fix me in place, the way I seem to be evading her.

'What is it?'

Anna stares back at me, withholding something. I notice that her eyes are ringed with red, the way mine must have looked at the party when she asked if I had been crying.

'I should just tell you…' she says.

'Tell me what?'

I can sense that she both does and doesn't want to say what is on her mind. She hesitates for a moment before speaking, her lip quivering.

'Luc broke up with me today.' Her eyes rapidly fill with tears. I make my way to the sofa and sit down beside her. Her whole body is shaking, and she begins to cry. I put my arms around her.

'Anna, I'm so sorry,' I say. I don't know what else to say; there's nothing else you *can* say. We're silent for a moment, as I hold her in my arms, and find that I do have one more thing to add:

'Everything's going to be okay,' I say — and I really do believe it.

We hug for a very long time. I become lost in listening to the birds chirping outside, and the soft sounds of traffic. Anna begins to breathe more deeply, her shaking gently subsiding.

'Why did he do it?' I ask her.

'Why do you think?'

'Because he's going to New York?'

Anna nods, the corners of her mouth turning down.

'I've been sitting up here all day waiting for you to come back,' she says, and I can't help but notice a hint of contempt in her voice.

'I'm sorry,' I say, 'you know I don't have a phone at the moment.' I hadn't bothered to purchase a new one since the incident on the viaduct. I realised that I didn't want to; the death of my phone had meant the death of many other things I didn't want in my life: my father, Olivier (and the others before him), and many more things I felt the possession of a phone made worse. I am enjoying living offline, and I feel more liberated than I have done in years because of it.

'Why don't you get a new one then? How long are you planning on not having a phone for?' I struggle to answer that question. 'How are you going to keep making plans with Val?' she persists. It's now impossible to ignore the resentment in her tone. She hates me being with Val. I tell her I'm going to my room, because I'm tired, which isn't completely untrue. I am just about to escape into the hallway when—

'I just think it's a little ironic,' she says. I stop in my tracks.

'What is?'

'You know what I mean. That things are actually going well with Val, considering…'

'Considering *what*?'

'You really want me to say it?' she threatens.

The silence hangs in the air between us. We both stare at each other like strangers. I feel us both unravelling, as if we are connected by the same thread, bound together only by a perpetual power struggle which she must always be winning.

'I didn't think so,' she says. Then she chuckles slowly. 'He'll discard you once he's bored with you. They always do.' I can't move. I feel tears prickling in my eyes which I blink desperately to keep away. 'And then you'll be back on this sofa with me.'

The more I try to blink back my tears, the faster they come. There is a sharp pain in my stomach, and I can see Anna regretting what she has said; she is going red in the cheeks, so red that I can almost feel the heat rising from them.

'Oh God…I'm so sorry. I—I—' she stammers, barely able to look me in the eye. She bursts into tears. 'I don't know why I said that.' It is only now that I remember she is drunk.

'It's okay,' I say, taking her wine glass over to the sink. Behind me I can hear her sobs becoming more emotional, more hysterical.

'We're just crazy, aren't we?' she says. 'Us women. Men just drive us crazy, then they leave.'

I pour the remainder of her wine down the sink, watching the dark red liquid swirl into the drain.

'The world is a dark, lonely place, isn't it?' Anna continues from the sofa. 'A tall, dark, lonely place.'

***

I am sat at my desk, with my notebook open in front of me. The words *Sacred Hearts* are scrawled in black ink at the top of the page, and I am tapping my pen against the desk, staring at them. It's no use. I simply don't want to write anymore; I am no longer unhappy. It's strange, I've never known an existence in which my writing has not been inextricably linked to my sadness, and now that sadness has been eradicated by the ecstasies of love, I'm out of words. I resent words, for all they fail to express when life transcends their dull, confining precision. Now the flame that had burned constantly within me has been extinguished in an instant. I pick up a lighter on my desk and begin to flick it, igniting the flame; on; then off; igniting; off; igniting… I eventually stop and put the lighter down, my eyes travelling to the window ahead. The huge shutters of the empty apartment across the street are wide open, gaping back at me. No one has lived there for six months now, and the place has taken on a melancholy air. I light a cigarette and watch it burn between my fingers, letting the ash fall onto the desk. I eventually put the cigarette in my mouth, but when I do almost choke because of what I see before me. His gaze catches me in its pathway and I can't look away. I blink but he's still at the window, watching me.

I scramble away from the desk, still feeling his shadowed eyes all over me, somehow getting closer. I shut the curtains, catching my breath. When I glimpse my reflection in the mirror I don't recognise myself at first, for all the colour is drained from my face.

***

I have decided to tell Val about the Tall Man, but he doesn't want to hear it. Sitting across from me in the Café St-Jean, his almond-shaped eyes scan mine with a level of concern I have never seen from him before; the kind of concern that we reserve only for those we are terrified of losing. This frightens me more, as I tell him about how I had seen the Tall Man in the empty apartment across the street.

'See, I knew you would look at me like that,' I say, trying to convince him I can make light of the situation; that I am not becoming untethered.

'Like what?'

'Like I've lost my mind.'

'No, not at all. It's just not what I was expecting to hear. Why do you think somebody's following you?'

Why indeed. Perhaps if I knew why, I wouldn't be so frightened about it. It is the unknown which is more terrifying than the being followed itself. I proceed to describe the Tall Man and his almost mythical presence; his long, black coat that evades decades, centuries even; his concealed face that belongs to no place or person; and his towering, aloof figure that anyone would find unnerving.

Val doesn't understand. How can he, when the dread I am describing can only be felt, not articulated?

***

It has been three days and Anna has disappeared. I am on the landline in the hall, trying to get hold of Val to tell him that she's gone, but he's not picking up. I have no doubt that the Tall Man is somehow connected. I don't want to be in the apartment by myself, so I go to a little bar at the end of the Rue de Bagnolet which seems to be stuck in the nineteen sixties, and it's making me feel sick. I ask to use their telephone, which is an old rotary phone stuck to the wall in faded cream plastic.

'Two minutes only,' says the bartender. I can feel her eyes piercing into the back of my head as I take the yellow Post-it note out of my bag which has Val and Anna's numbers on it. I call Anna first. I know she's not going to answer, but I leave a message anyway. I tell her to come to the bar, and in the same breath I already know she won't. Then I call Val. He doesn't answer either.

'What's the strongest drink you've got?' I ask the bartender.

I get home drunk a couple of hours later, struggling to get my key in the door. I drank nearly a whole bottle of wine at the bar, avoiding the cruel glances of strangers who must have been wondering what I was doing there alone, draining a bottle of red with a sullen expression on my face, constructing some tragic narrative for me, oblivious to the nightmare I am living.

I finally get the front door open and fall against the frame like one of those old men you see in the alleyways late at night, muttering profanities to passersby, reeking of urine and alcohol. I switch on the light, close the door and drop my keys onto the side table. I check Anna's room, but she's not there. I lie down on my bed and pass out.

***

It's morning now and I am trying to call Val. I'm supposed to be meeting him tonight to see the première of *Ville de Nuit*, the film whose poster I had seen plastered around Paris ever since the night I met Val. We decided to look up the film after I'd pointed the poster out, and it transpired that *Ville de Nuit* just so happened to be having its première at Le Voile cinema. It was hard to think of this as just another coincidence, but more as a synchronicity, with everything else that was happening. Of course, I was utterly compelled to attend the première, so we had managed to get a couple of guest tickets through the Paris School of Cinema. But now Val is not answering his phone. I leave him a message, and I sound frightened, lost…

I don't know where Anna is. I don't know where you are. Are you together? I'm really worried. If I don't hear back from you...well I'll assume you're still meeting me tonight. And if I don't see you then...I don't know. Please come tonight. Please.

Now I am on my way to Le Voile. I feel ridiculous in this silk black dress, my lips the colour of the circus, my face suffocating behind a wall of makeup. I hope he is there, waiting for me. All of a sudden I am overwhelmed by how much I love him, of how all I want in this moment is to feel his lips against mine, and the soft strap of my dress falling down...down...

I cross the road absentmindedly, cars slowing rapidly as I realise the lights are red and that I shouldn't be crossing. An aggressive car horn jolts me to the other side of the road, and I tell myself to keep it together, *please, Marie,* just for tonight.

He is there, under the cinema canopy. The relief is so intoxicating that I can hardly walk, and I have to blink to make sure he is real, that Val is truly here, dressed in a light brown suit and smoking a cigarette. As I near the cinema, my attention is drawn to a subtle noise creeping through the general ambience. It is a lighter flicking. I try to figure out where it is coming from, searching the shadows beneath the canopy. I am sure that it must mean something, but I don't know why. Then I see it: the flame ignites the tip of a cigarette at the far end of the canopy, and I can see exactly who it belongs to. I scream. A number of people stop and stare; I can feel a hundred eyes on me; Val comes running forward, grabbing my hands.

'Marie! Are you okay?' he says, horrified. I point in the direction of the canopy.

'He's there!'

Val looks behind him. A clique of fashionable people in evening dresses and suits are staring at us. The Tall Man has vanished.

'Who's there?'

'The Tall Man. He was there. He was right there, lighting a cigarette…I heard his lighter…he's following me…'

I sound like a lunatic, but I can't help it; he has got me pinned between two worlds, struggling to inhabit either, constantly waking up out of one nightmare and into another, as if my dream had never really ended. Val places his hands on my shoulders, and once again I am transported back to the fantasy of my dress strap falling down. I imagine ourselves in the park when the weather is hot, and he is undressing me slowly, kissing the smooth skin of my shoulder, his hand pressed against the inside of my thigh, pushing me down on the grass…

'Marie, look at me,' he says; but all I can think is that I don't want to be here. Why must the fantasy always remain an inch out of reach?

'Why didn't you answer my calls?'

Val looks at me in confusion.

'What calls?'

'I left you three messages,' I say. 'Didn't you get them?'

'No, I didn't,' he replies. I don't know what he is thinking, but it can't be good. 'Come here,' he says, wrapping his arms around me and stroking the back of my head.

'I left messages. Anna's gone.'

'What do you mean, Anna's gone?'

'She's gone missing. She hasn't been in the apartment for three days and I can't get hold of her. I don't know where she's gone. She hasn't returned any of my calls.'

I watch the guests file into the cinema, effortlessly chic, as if plucked from the latest issue of *Vogue*.

'Can we just go in?' I implore Val. I don't want to think about Anna anymore.

The lobby is filled with graceful women and suited men. Waiters carry trays of canapés and Champagne, as the rattle of laughter and exaggerated greetings fills the air. Posters for *Ville de Nuit* adorn the walls, as the guests walk up to them, curiously pondering their image; the solitary woman on the balcony, the orange lights of the city reaching out to meet the Eiffel Tower, an impossible pylon of wrought iron and skeleton dreams.

We blend into the crowd, minus a few strange looks from those who saw the commotion outside. Thankfully there was no one guarding the door. A waiter comes over to offer us a glass of Champagne, which we both accept.

'*Santé,*' says Val, and we clink our glasses together. He can tell I am uneasy, so he puts his arms around me. I move away from his embrace.

'I don't want to think about it anymore,' I say. 'I want to watch the film.' I know I sound like an impertinent child, but Val nods anyway, knowing it is probably better to keep his mouth shut. I raise the glass of Champagne to my lips and down the whole thing.

'All better,' I say, with a smile that feels like I am being torn apart from the inside.

As we pass back into the crowd of forty or so people, I think I can see the silver-haired man from before; the man I had seen when my father had rung from England, who was speaking to the woman by the door. It is definitely the same man.

'That's the director,' Val says. I turn and look at Val, not believing my ears.

'What?'

'The man with the silver hair. He's Jacques Beaudet.'

I have moved beyond fear now, past distress for Anna, and am consumed with fascination. I don't know what compels me, but I find myself angling my face and my body in a way that might attract his gaze. I need to meet him, to find out why fate has brought us here. Now I know for certain that there is some greater force at play. Our eyes meet. He smiles at me, and I can sense Val's confusion as he fidgets with his Champagne glass.

I take a fresh glass from a passing waiter. I watch as Jacques Beaudet says goodbye to someone and approaches us.

'*Bonsoir*,' he says, his voice arresting and sonorous, like a magician about to perform his main trick.

'*Bonsoir*,' we both reply.

'Pardon me for interrupting,' he says, 'but Mademoiselle, we have met before?'

I feel my cheeks flushing red. Jacques takes my hand and brings it to his lips; they are very warm and soft, I can't help but notice.

'No, I don't think so,' I say.

'Oh…' he replies, a hint of surprise in his tone. 'I thought — I thought you looked familiar.'

'You must have me mistaken with someone else.'

'Evidently. Well, it's a pleasure to meet you. I'm Jacques.'

'Marie.'

'Marie,' he repeats slowly, as if it is the most exquisite sound he has ever heard. '*Enchanté*.' He takes my hand again.

'I'm Val,' Val suddenly interjects.

Jacques takes only the slightest notice of him, as if paying him any more than the bare minimum attention would somehow tarnish his reputation; Val is surely hurt by this. I, however, have nearly finished my second glass of Champagne, and it has gone straight to my head.

'What brings you both to my première tonight?' Jacques asks us.

'Fate,' I say, without even thinking about it. I can tell Jacques is intrigued.

'We're both aspiring filmmakers,' Val qualifies, 'I'm a huge admirer of your work.'

Jacques smiles politely at Val, and then goes back to ignoring him; but before we can talk further, a man in a suit comes and taps Jacques on the shoulder, gesturing to the auditorium.

'*Fate?*' Val hisses under his breath.

***

I wake up crying and drenched in a cold sweat. I do not know what day it is or what has happened, or if any of the events of the past twenty-four hours were real. My room is the same; the white curtains, the bedsheets, *Good Morning, Midnight* on my bedside table, my film posters, my records — it is all there; it is all there, but none of it feels right.

Last night I dreamed I was lost in a thick layer of fog, so dense I couldn't see through it. It whirled slowly in a menacing display, inviting me into a deathlike embrace with its ghostly tendrils. Gradually the fog began to thin, disclosing the outlines of the viaduct upon which I stood, and the hazy nothingness which lay beyond. The sky was tinged with a dark purple hue that signalled neither day nor night. It was only when I looked down at my hands that I realised they were the hands of a child, and I was in the body of my younger self.

I walked along the bridge, which only seemed to stretch out further each time a mass of fog cleared. I don't know how long I walked for, but just when I began to think there would be no end to the road, I saw a figure in the distance. It was a young woman in a white dress, looking out over the stretch of purple-grey gloom. It was my mother.

She stepped up to the balustrade, her face calm as she stood before the vacuous mist beneath her, looking straight down. I began running towards her, but the fog only thickened, and I became lost in it; each time I tried to run in one direction, I came up against an even thicker curtain of fog. I would try over and over to change direction, only to be confronted with nothing. I kept spinning in circles, gaining in speed until I could not separate left from right. It was only when I was on the point of falling over that I saw the Tall Man's figure materialising in the distance, coming towards me. I thought that at some point he would stop walking, but he only got closer, until he was so near that I began to see his face for the first time. In that moment, I was filled with something I can only describe as a deep sense of the uncanny. He had the face of my father, only he had aged horribly, gaunt and cadaverous, his eyes great black stones set within withered skin that hung loosely from his cheeks, his mouth a thin, straight line which betrayed no emotion. He stopped about a metre away, towering over me. Behind him, the fog revealed my mother once again. I was too scared to run towards her now, for fear of what my father might do. He was watching me, trying to intimidate me as my mother flirted with the massive drop beneath the viaduct.

The fog curled around her body, and I watched unflinchingly as she put one foot over the precipice and fell suddenly, almost peacefully, into the void. Then I woke up.

I am in the kitchen now, where Val is making crêpes. Anna is still not here. There is a jar of fresh marigolds on the windowsill, and Françoise Hardy's *Tous les garçons et les filles* is issuing from the record player. The smell of fresh coffee assaults my senses, and everything is too familiar. This exceeds *déjà-vu*. I wonder if I am still dreaming.

'Morning,' Val says casually, as if nothing unusual has ever happened.

I stand in the doorway, my head a swirling disarray of dreams, paranoia and that astringent smell of coffee that follows you everywhere in Paris. 'Crêpe?' he holds out the pan to me, with a perfectly formed, golden brown pancake inside.

'What the fuck is going on?' I demand to know. Val cowers.

'…I thought you might want something to eat.'

I stumble back into the hallway, and retreat to my room, but Val follows me and makes me talk to him.

'What happened last night?' I say.

Val tells me I blacked out at Jacques' première after the opening credits; he tells me how scared he was and how he called us a taxi because he didn't know what else to do, and thought I might have been drugged. But I don't believe him.

I know immediately I can't trust anything anyone says, and when I look down at my hand I notice that it is shaking. I have a sensation that I'm continually falling; that metal ball has returned to the pit of my stomach, pulling me down, I don't know where…Val must know. He must know what's going to happen—

'He's coming to get me,' I say. I know he is.

'No he's not!' Val replies, and all I hear is *shut up*.

'Yes he is. First it was the dream, then the Sacré-Coeur, then—'

'You saw him at the Sacré-Coeur?' Val interjects.

I think about it again. Did I see the Tall Man outside the Sacré-Coeur? I thought I did. I don't know. I think I did—he was standing down there on the grass when the bells struck twelve, that was why I almost fell…

'Yes — the night we met…why did you think I was so scared?' I say.

'Why didn't you tell me this before? You can't just go around adding new details whenever you feel like it!'

Did I add a new detail? My brain is so mixed up I don't know anymore. Did I drink coffee yesterday morning? Did I see the film last night? My whole life spins around me like a record being flung out into space. I think I saw him, but I don't know.

'I'm not adding new details!' I insist. Val softens his tone.

'Marie…I don't know what's happened here, but…I just want you to be okay. This man…' he falls silent. I stare at him, trying to ignore the subtle shaking of my limbs. 'I say this with only good intent, but…have you ever…*spoken* to anyone about your past?'

'You mean a psychiatrist?' I spit these words out like they're poison. 'Are you fucking serious?'

Suddenly Val slams his hand onto the bed and I flinch. It reminds me of when my father used to hit things in fits of rage. One time, he punched his thin, sharp knuckles into a wall, leaving a blood-encrusted ring above our television.

'Jesus Christ, I'm trying to help you!' Val yells at me. *Fuck him*, I think. I can't help it. I am shaking with rage, sadness and a mistrust that I don't want to have. I can't bear the silence, so I get up and leave.

I am running down the street, so fast that Val can't possibly catch up. I run continuously until I get to the nearest Métro stop and descend into the cool, dark labyrinth of train lines which can take me anywhere. I hop on Ligne 2 and change at Jaurés. I know where I am headed now.

When I ascend back out into the bright streets it is surprisingly quiet. Not a person or a car is in sight. I walk a little further until I find myself back at Le Voile. The giant posters for *Ville de Nuit* are still in the windows.

The cinema lobby is nearly empty, with just a couple of staff members at the bar, and an elderly man drinking coffee by the window. I wait until the staff are not looking, then I slip into the auditorium from last night. There is no one inside. The lights are dim, the screen blank. I let the door fall shut behind me, giving way to total silence. I am here because I want to remember what happened last night.

I go and sit in an empty seat, watching the black, vacant screen. The silence is enveloping and oppressive. I still remember the first ten minutes or so of the film; they were bizarre and anachronistic, belonging to the era of Hitchcock, not today. There had been one suspenseful scene, where the lead actress — who had the same hair as me, but a much prettier face — entered a darkened room where objects loomed in the shadows and deep sounds permeated the space; in the corner of the room there had been a faint figure—

The auditorium door opens. I panic and turn to see who's there. The Riviera-tanned face of Jacques Beaudet regards me curiously.

'Oh — hello,' he says, hovering awkwardly in the threshold. For once I see his vulnerability, his self-consciousness an unwanted aura in this darkened room, where he must think I am a crazed fan, come back here just to relive the night.

'Hi—I'm sorry, I didn't mean to—' I stammer stupidly.

'You enjoyed the film that much, did you?' I'm relieved he can make a joke out of it. I quickly think of an excuse which will make me sound less insane.

'I was just…I came to pick up my purse.'

'Oh — did you find it?'

'Yes — yes, it was just under the seat.'

A silence passes between us as Jacques steps into the room and the door closes on us. He clears his throat, and I realise my awkwardness is making him uncomfortable. I must try and shed my present doubts to inhabit a new self, one that will smile and laugh at the right moments, and captivate her listeners rather than making them uneasy or bored. The suggestion of this other self appears like a siren on the rocks, luring me to her song. Perhaps I can be this other woman.

'I was just coming back to look for my cigarette case,' Jacques says.

I offer to help him find it, and he is pleased when I discover a small gold box lying beneath one of the seats in the front row. It has an enamel painting on the lid, depicting a tall, cloaked figure ascending a set of stairs, wilted flower in hand. I find it oddly fascinating. I hand Jacques his case.

'This case is very important to me. It has been in my family for generations,' he says. I can't stop staring at it. He notices me eyeing the case and opens it.

'Cigarette?'

We go to a nearby café and order a pichet of wine. I have allowed myself to become possessed by a new Marie — Marie from Paris, who drinks wine at noon with strange men, whose laughter rings with the power of nonchalance and indifference towards the world — I feel like an entirely different person, and it is exhilarating.

Jacques has picked the most intimate table outside the café, where the light gently touches our faces and wine glasses, illuminating Jacques' flawless silver hair. Closer up, the lines on his face are more pronounced and telling of his age. I would guess he is forty-eight. His cigarette case sits on the table, and I am still entranced by it. I have a persistent thought in the back of my mind that the image must mean something.

Jacques questions me about Val, trying to find out how serious we are about each other. I have got to keep my cool and seem easy about this. It's not that I want to seduce him as such, but to dabble with the city itself, to find out what it means to be a true Parisian — and I realise that the essence of what I want in life lies simply in not caring. It lies in not giving a damn about what happened before I came here, and in not even attempting to erase that past. I sink into this newly discovered side of myself like a second skin.

We talk for a long time — about film school, and how Jacques didn't go because he didn't think you could teach creativity; we spoke about being young and feeling invincible (which I have never felt before, until now); and about free will versus fate. We move onto another bar and order another pichet of wine; I get quite drunk, and forget all about Anna, the Tall Man, my dreams and everything else.

Two hours later I am in Jacques' apartment in Montmartre, feeling more gregarious than I have in months; and although I am wracked with guilt about leaving Val this morning, I'm filled with a more urgent desire to let go of everything. I lean back into Jacques' couch, as Django Reinhardt's *Hommage à Debussy* crackles from the speakers. His living room is filled with obscure film posters and modernist art, with arcane books on philosophy and psychology littering the coffee table and shelves.

'So, you want to be an *auteur*,' Jacques says, lighting another cigarette.

'I hope to be.'

'You are writing a script?'

'Yes.'

'Is it for your degree? Or in your spare time?'

'It's for school, but also in my spare time.'

'Good,' he replies, almost sternly. 'Those are the only kinds of projects we as artists should be working on. You know we have a social responsibility not to sell out.' I wonder who this unified 'we' is, for he and I are certainly not the same. 'Once you start selling out, you stop speaking your truth, and you start following orders. You maintain a status quo that no real artist can fully reconcile with their desire to create.'

'Yes…that's true,' I respond weakly. This conversation can't go on; it is far too serious and calculated for my liking. I'm sure he has said this to every young woman who has sunk into this couch, and stared at the writings of Freud on the table, feeling her blood warm with excitement and unease. I see myself lying on a psychoanalyst's couch, Jacques' face scrutinising mine from behind a pair of round spectacles.

I wonder what character he will write me into next, as he mines my soul for details.

'Am I radicalising you?' he says. I want to laugh; he thinks that he can have a real impact on me, looking at me as if I were an empty book waiting to be written.

'You think I'm naïve,' I say, smiling. He is eyeing me curiously; he knows that there is more to my story than I am willing to disclose.

'How old are you?' he demands to know.

'I'm twenty-one,' but I say it like I'm twenty-seven.

He refills my wine glass, then moves his profoundly dark eyes over my face, trying to find something, some small detail, to latch onto.

'You have been disappointed in matters of the heart,' he says. I wonder if this is a simple guess, or if it is really that obvious.

'In the past, yes.'

'You must have asked yourself before, *Why me? Why should this happen to me?*'

I don't reply; I want to go back to Val, but it is too late, and I have a glass full of wine in my hand. I contemplate throwing it at Jacques, but I want Marie from Paris to play along with this charade for as long as she can. As long as I can live her life, I don't have to go back to mine.

'What if I told you there is no answer to that question?' Jacques continues.

'I already knew that,' I say.

Why is the only question worth asking, my father's voice seeps into the room through a crack in the ceiling; a quiet and lethal whisper that only I can hear.

'Then why do we ask it at all?' Jacques says.

Because it is the only question worth asking.

I don't like this; I can feel my father's presence all around us in this sealed, unholy space, entangling us in his web of unanswered questions. I need to find some way to exorcise him, but all I can say is:

'Do all questions need to be answered?'

I miss Val now and his gentle, almond eyes; I miss the softness of his lips against mine, like an unfurling petal in the rose-coloured dawn; I miss the steady, rhythmic vibrations of his heart beating, as I lay my head on his chest and feel — not think; I miss the daylight outside.

***

By the time I get home it is nearly seven o'clock in the morning. Marie from Paris has dissolved into the remnants of last night's wine, and I walk as a ghost in my own town. I go straight to my room and curl up in a ball on my bed, ashamed of myself.

I am trying to piece together what has happened over the past few days — weeks, even — but it only half makes sense to me; there are missing pieces to the puzzle that are yet to be placed, and I am at the centre of it. And although the image does not yet make sense, I'm certain that it will in time.

It is funny how when you think of the unity of life, your thoughts can easily turn towards death. I think about death in this moment, and it feels astonishingly close; I can feel its breath, caressing my arms, pulling me towards an unknown destination. I am not scared of this sensation, and I never have been. It has always been there waiting for me, as I lay down under the great oak tree at university, feeling the warm grass poke through the fabric of my top; it is there when I stop to watch the water run out of the tap, a miniature stream in my own kitchen, that settles in the bottom of the sink, its own Lilliputian lake; it is there where I close my eyes at night, waiting for me, not asking me to come, but welcoming me nonetheless. And yet we are born to fear it. As if nothing could hurt us more than nothing.

My thoughts are interrupted by a sudden, deafening bang from the kitchen. I open my eyes and sit up, my heart palpitating. I stand to face the door but am paralysed beyond this point, fearing that if I so much as move, something terrible will happen. I wait, as the faint sound of music travels from the kitchen and through the hallway, finally creeping under the door…Françoise Hardy's *Tous les garçons et les filles*. I recoil at the singer's dreamy lamentations of love, abjuring any sense of peace with death that I had just now, and fearing for my life. I know that this is intended for me, that I must go and investigate whatever lies on the other side of the door. *Dear God*, I think, in spite of my lack of belief, *please protect me*.

Standing in the kitchen, I think I must be dreaming. But each time I blink, the image doesn't go away. Blood spills across the breakfast counter, climbing over the edges and dripping down into crimson pools on the floor. Anna's body is collapsed over it, her hair matted with all kinds of things that no human eye should ever see. The revolver is still in her right hand. I violently shudder as I realise what is happening. My own hand comes over my mouth like a gag; I can't bear it.

I stumble backwards, losing my balance and hitting the door frame, but my eyes won't let go of the scene. On the counter next to Anna lies a piece of folded paper — a note. My attention swerves between the note, the revolver, and Anna, slumped over the counter like a deflated balloon, blood trickling out from all angles. I want to read the note, but

I know what is in it will be designed to unhinge me further from reality, this city, from all of life. I have also learnt by now that all I can do is follow these leads, which may or may not draw me to their inevitable conclusion. I unfold the note, my hands trembling. It reads: *You said everything was going to be okay.* I cast my mind back to when I said these words, cradling Anna on the sofa as she cried over Luc, wondering if that is what she meant. What is written afterwards is more concerning:

I wish I was dead
I wish I was dead
I wish I was dead
I wish I was dead
I wish I was dead

The letters blur into a jumbled mess on the page as I stare right through them, struggling to breathe. This was not how the dream was supposed to end; what twisted shoes did she click together when she whispered this cold refrain? And how on earth did she get hold of that gun? *I wish I was dead.*

A loud buzz from the hallway cuts through everything. It is the front door. The music on the record player is still going, and I don't bother to turn it off. Instead I panic, and go to the intercom.

'Hello?' I say.

I am met with silence.

'Hello?' I wait again for a reply, but there isn't one.

I know he is coming for me now. I am about to go back to the kitchen when I hear footsteps beginning to echo up the stairwell. They come closer, as the record slowly dies out.

They are a man's footsteps, slow and solemn. They stop outside the apartment, and I instinctively take a step back. He knocks on the front door. I don't know what to do in this moment, so I stand very still, listening. There is an unnerving silence that just won't settle. Another knock.

I approach the door, feeling like I could almost die on the spot, awaiting my fate. I open the door and stare in disbelief at the face of Val, choking on my own tears. Without a word between us, I fling my arms around him, and he hugs me back tightly. I don't know how long we embrace for, but when we pull away I feel confused and sad, as if Anna were the real victim of the Tall Man, and her death was merely the cost of my happiness.

'Where have you been?' says Val. 'I tried calling, but you weren't picking up — I've been so worried.' I don't know what to say, because I can't tell him the truth, nor can I bear to lie. He simply kisses the top of my head, holding me in his arms like a small child. 'Don't scare me like that again, Marie,' he says.

I continue to cry, softly at first, but my tears soon grow into uncontrollable sobs. Val pulls away and searches my face.

'What is it?'

I look towards the kitchen door.

'What is it?' he repeats.

Anna is still draped over the breakfast counter. At my back I hear Val's breath grow shaky, as he barely musters the word *what*...Neither of us can string a sentence together. I try to explain how I heard the gunshot, and then the music, and how I somehow knew this might happen, even though *how could I possibly have known*, and a hundred other words which fall to the ground without making an impact.

'Where did the gun come from?' Val asks, staring at the revolver on the counter.

I look at it too, and realise that I don't even need to think about it; I just remember Val saying one radiant morning, his hands clasped behind his head as he lay on my bed, that in French New Wave films everybody has a gun. He looks up at me and appears to realise it too. Did we really unwittingly transform our lives into a film? Is this the denouement? But it is impossible to see things that way; for the stories of our lives are more than acts in a film — and how could we be nearing the end, when everything makes so little sense? Val moves closer to me and embraces me again.

'Everything is going to be okay.'

I freeze as he says this. How could he have picked those precise words at this moment? How could he have said them, and not known they were the same words written on the crumpled note in my pocket? I am suddenly without a doubt that Val is part of the Tall Man's plot. It all makes sense; I had never even seen Val before that day in May, the same day I had dreamed of the Tall Man the night before; the same day my father had called from England to reel me back into the past; the same day I had thrown my phone off a bridge and cut off my connection with the rest of the world; the same day I had seen the Tall Man weave through the blurry crowd of passengers on the Métro; the same day that I was given a second chance in life. Val is the Tall Man. I see it now.

I start beating his chest to get him away, but he won't let go. He smells like fresh coffee and cigarettes and it's making me nauseous. I keep on hitting him with my fists, imagining that if I keep going, he will eventually dissipate into nothing. The rhythm of my fists gradually slows as my hands become weak; I find that I am no longer supported by Val's body, and I fall to the floor.

When I look up, Val has vanished into thin air. I look around in terror. Anna's blood is spreading out into a wider pool, painting the floorboards dark red. There is a soft weight in both of my palms, and when I look down at them, there are two small piles of ash in each hand. They are already slipping through my fingers onto the floor, and I know at this point that Marie from Paris is embedded in those ashes; a pale memory of what once was, of desires unmet, dreams unfulfilled, of a hopeless vision of a city that I had failed in realising. I wait until the ash is scattered completely around my knees before I look up again. When I do, sure enough, the Tall Man is there, waiting for me with his faceless stare. He extends out a black gloved hand and beckons me to follow him. I can hardly refuse.

The Tall Man gestures to my kitchen door, which leads to the hallway. I follow him, but once across the threshold, I find myself in Square Louise-Michel. It is nighttime, and the street lamps glow a dull yellow, the place deserted and humid, as if it might rain heavily. I am looking up at the white steps leading to the Sacré-Coeur. The Tall Man is nowhere to be seen, but he has left something in my hand — a wilted marigold. I remember Jacques' cigarette case, and the cloaked figure on the steps, holding the dead flower, and realise why I had been so entranced by this image. I hear footsteps behind me and turn to see who it is. At a short distance someone is coming towards me. A young woman with a bob; I peer closer and watch the pensive sway in her step, her unfamiliarity with her own place in the world, and I realise that this young woman is me. She is wearing the same clothes from the night I met Val. Drawing closer, my double takes no notice of me, but simply walks past, up the steps. I follow her. Her movements are slow and wavering, like someone who is unsure of where they are headed. When I get to the top, I watch this other self go and sit on the parapet, overlooking the wide and ceaseless sea of lights beyond, a late night fairy kingdom for the anonymous drifter. But I am quite certain now of her destination. She closes her eyes, and I watch as she lets the breeze caress her hair. When she speaks, her voice trembles with despair.

'Please give me a sign,' she says.

At that precise moment, the church bells from the Sacré-Coeur begin to toll. This is the sign. And to my horror, I see her stand up tall on the parapet, her arms open against the sky like a majestic bird. The bells continue to toll, and I glimpse a familiar figure sweep across the platform below — a rush of darkness under a hat. I watch myself step off the parapet.

***

I can hardly breathe. Blood spreads across the pool, illuminated by the lights, turning the water from turquoise to scarlet. I want to look away, but I feel compelled to stare at the cracked head, the petrified face, the big blue eyes gaping back at me in terror, the open mouth with downturned lips. Her face reminds me of a carnival mask, with heavily painted eyes and perfect skin. She is both beautiful and hideous at the same time.

I can only guess at what her last thoughts might have been; but what use is this guessing now? I didn't know her and I never will. If only I had been more prepared, I might have. But what is the use in all this speculation?

'Val!' Anna calls from behind me. I turn around; she is just coming to the top of the steps with Luc.

'Is she up here?'

ACKNOWLEDGEMENTS

I'm aware that all I have talked about for the past six years is some variation of this story — so first of all, thank you to everyone who has ever sat through me doing this and responded with some form of encouragement. A huge thank you goes to Philip Palmer, Julian Henriques and everybody on the Goldsmiths MA Scriptwriting course, who helped me workshop Sacred Hearts into a screenplay; I went back and revisited the novella after that, and a lot of valuable feedback made its way into the prose.

Another big thank you goes to Robin L. Finetto, who read countless drafts of this book over the years, and has been an integral part of the creative evolution of this story. Thank you to Nathan Newman, who read one of the later drafts of this story and told me to scrap all of the backstory stuff and to make it longer — sorry Nathan! A huge, huge thank you to Suzanne Escaig for your unwavering support and friendship throughout the production of this novella. Thank you for encouraging me to translate such complex personal experiences into art.

Thanks also to: My parents and siblings (and Em); Emily Louise Church; Sam Kohn; Sam Greaves; Hoagy Hickson; Carys Maloney; Madeleine Clench; guy I went on a date with in 2022 who asked for the manuscript (bit awkward but I hope you enjoyed it?); Goldsmiths, University of London; and to anyone who has ever supported and read my work over the years. Your readership means the world.

Printed in Great Britain
by Amazon